Mum, You're Fired!

by NANCY K. ROBINSON
Illustrated by ED ARNO

SCHOLASTIC BOOK SERVICES

NEW YORK · TORONTO · LONDON · AUCKLAND · SYDNEY · TOKYO

To Peter . . .

0-590-72093-7

Text copyright © 1981 by Nancy K. Robinson. Illustrations copyright © 1981 by Scholastic Inc. All rights reserved. Published by Scholastic Book Services, a division of Scholastic Inc.

12 11 10 9 8 7 6 5 4 3 2 1   3   1 2 3 4 5 6/8
Printed in the U. S. A.   01

Commonwealth Edition

The Long Bus Ride

"Is this the bus to Davenport Street?" Tina's mother called up to the bus driver but he didn't seem to hear her.

Tina's mother stepped up on to the bus. She was carrying two shopping bags under one arm and Tina's little sister Angela under the other arm. Angela twisted around until she was almost hanging upside down.

"New shoes," said Angela to the man at the back of her, pointing proudly to her new white shoes. "Much too esspensive," she added.

Tina and her brother Nathaniel looked at each other. Then they stepped back in the line and let two ladies get in front of them. They each had their own bus fare and wanted to get as far away from their mother and their little sister as possible.

Then they heard their mother ask in an even louder voice:

"Driver, I asked if this was the bus to Davenport Street."

"Read the sign, lady," they heard the bus driver shout.

"The sign outside the bus is stuck," their mother said crossly.

There was no answer from the bus driver.

"Hurry up, lady," called a man at the end of the bus line.

But their mother wasn't in any hurry. She was giving the bus driver a lecture.

"...and the least you could do is tell me whether or not I'm on the right bus. It would only be common courtesy..."

"Oh, no." Nathaniel grabbed Tina's arm. "Here she goes again." He pulled Tina back and let a boy carrying a large transistor radio get in front of them.

"Look, lady," shouted the bus driver. "Are you getting on or off? I don't have all day."

Everyone in the line was very quiet.

Tina stared hard at a crack in the footpath. She felt like pulling her mother off the bus and shaking her.

"Move on, lady," the man at the back of the line called again.

"It's the right bus," a lady called out. "It's a number 8. This one goes to Davenport Street."

"Thank you." Tina's mother turned around and nodded to the lady. "But I don't see why the bus driver couldn't have told me that. If I had a choice, I wouldn't even take this bus."

Nathaniel groaned. "Why can't she just get on the bus and be quiet like everyone else?"

Slowly the line of people began to move ahead.

"Nathaniel, Christina, are you there?" Now their mother was inside the bus, pounding on the window and waving at them. Tina and Nathaniel pretended not to notice.

As they were paying their fare, they saw a man get up and give their mother his seat. Tina and Nathaniel tried to squeeze to the rear of the bus, but it was too crowded to move. They were stuck right across the aisle from their mother, who had Angela on her lap.

"New shoes," said Angela to everyone who passed by.

Nathaniel grabbed on to a pole and began to read an advertisement posted above the window.

YOU TOO CAN BE A
NATURAL BLONDE OR REDHEAD

Tina held on to the same pole and stared out of the window.

"There's a package missing," their mother suddenly gasped.

Tina and Nathaniel heard the rustling of paper bags.

"It was a white paper bag with red stripes. The one with all the underwear in it," wailed their mother.

Tina looked at Nathaniel. But now he was busy reading an advertisement for life insurance as if it were the most interesting thing he had ever read. He was bright pink around the ears.

"Underwear!" shouted Angela. She giggled and clapped her hands. "Where's the underwear?" She poked her head under the seat, trying to help her mother look.

The bus was very crowded, but everyone seemed especially quiet this Saturday afternoon. All Tina could hear was her mother rustling through paper bags.

"Here it is," she called out happily.

Tina held her breath. She prayed that her mother would not say the word "underwear" again. Her mother didn't say it. The lady sitting next to her did.

"Oh, I'm so glad you found the children's

underwear. It's so expensive nowadays."

"We've just bought it," Tina's mother explained. Tina peered at her mother.

To her horror she saw her mother taking out the underwear — piece by piece — to make sure it was all there: Tina's new flowered pants, Nathaniel's jockey shorts, Angela's tiny vests, and her mother's enormous bra.

Tina tried to make herself very thin so she could hide behind a pole. The lady was still talking to her mother.

"They wear it out so quickly."

"Especially in summer," Tina's mother agreed. It was now the middle of September.

Nathaniel leaned over and whispered angrily in Tina's ear, "Can you believe it? She has the whole bus discussing our underwear. It's so *humiliating!*"

Nathaniel was eleven. He was two years older than Tina, and she was always impressed when he used grown-up words like "humiliating."

The bus stopped. A few people got out. It was less crowded, but Tina and Nathaniel were still trapped a short distance from their mother.

"Well, at least I don't have to worry about

nappies for this one anymore," their mother said, pointing to Angela.

"Dirty nappies are awful," said Angela to the strange lady.

Now Tina began to read the advertisement for hair colour. She didn't want to hear what her mother and the lady were saying about toilet training. She wondered if she should dye her hair bright red. Then no one would guess that she was related to anyone in her family. Everyone in her family had dark-brown hair.

"What nice new shoes," the lady next to her mother said. Well, at least she could talk about something besides underwear.

Angela leaned over and stared straight into the lady's eyes. "Much too esspensive," she said very seriously. "We can't afford them." Then she said slowly, "Fourteen hundred and ninety-eight dollars."

"My, my," said the lady.

"Fourteen dollars and ninety-eight cents." Tina's mother brushed off Angela's shoes. Even she seemed a little embarrassed.

"Isn't she sweet?" said the lady. "And how old are you?"

Tina didn't have to look to know that Angela was going through her same old act.

She always put up one, two, three and a half fingers.

"My, my," said the lady again. "Three and a half years old."

The bus stopped again. More people got out, including the underwear lady. Tina and Nathaniel found a seat at the back of the bus.

As the bus started up again, they both heard their mother begin to hum.

She didn't hum like other people. She always hummed opera. Soon the hum became "Tra...la...la..." Tina and Nathaniel stared out of the window. Their mother's voice seemed to be getting louder and louder.

"How many more stops?" asked Nathaniel desperately.

Tina counted. "Six, I think."

"La . . . la . . . la la la . . . tra . . . la . . . la." Tina's mother had studied to be an opera singer before she was married.

The people on the bus were very quiet.

"Now," Angela suddenly piped up in her loud baby voice.

Her mother stopped singing. "What, dear?"

"Now," Angela said again. She was sitting on her mother's lap swinging her feet back and forth.

"Let's see how many people on this bus are

fat." Angela clasped her hands and studied all the people on the bus.

"There's that lady over there. She's fat," she said, pointing.

"Shhh," her mother said.

"And that man," said Angela. "He's as fat as a house."

Tina's mother suddenly burst out singing again. Words and everything. She didn't even sing in English. Meanwhile, Angela kept counting fat people. She had to count in an even louder voice so that she could hear herself above her mother's singing.

The bus ride was the longest one Tina could remember. As soon as the bus pulled into the Davenport Street stop, Tina and Nathaniel got off the bus in a hurry and ran ahead.

"Wait for us," their mother called. "Wait at the corner."

When Tina and Nathaniel reached the corner, they stopped. Tina hid behind a tree.

She hid behind a tree because her best friend Melissa lived in a brownstone house across the street. Tina hoped that no one in Melissa's house was looking out of the window just now.

Melissa was very lucky. Her mother was

perfect. Melissa's mother had her hair done once a week and always wore tweed suits with white silk blouses. She was president of the PTA and had a schedule every day — meetings, appointments, errands . . . Tina always read Mrs. Glenn's schedule when she went to visit Melissa. It was posted on the kitchen wall next to the stove.

Tina watched her mother and Angela coming up the street. Her mother's blouse wasn't even tucked in all the way around and she was missing a button on her skirt.

Tina peered around the tree to make sure no one was looking out of the windows of Melissa's house. The neat white curtains were closed behind the flower boxes that stood in each window. Melissa's mother was very active in the Flower Box Programme to make the street beautiful.

Tina breathed a sigh of relief. She was pretty sure Melissa's family was away for the weekend.

"Hi, Tina."

Tina whirled around.

"Oh, hi," she said. She felt foolish. Why did she have to meet someone she knew? It was Sarah who was new this year in her class.

Sarah was playing jacks alone on the footpath in front of a big apartment block.

"You live here?" asked Tina nervously. She hadn't known that Sarah lived right across the street from Melissa.

"Uh huh," said Sarah.

Out of the corner of her eye, Tina saw her mother and Angela getting closer. Her mother was dragging Angela, who kept stopping every few metres to brush off her new white shoes.

Why did her mother have to wear that blue-flowered scarf tied around her head? She looked like a gypsy with her long dangling earrings. She was still singing.

"Is that your mother?"

"Huh?" asked Tina.

"Is that lady your mother?" asked Sarah.

Tina looked all around pretending she didn't know to whom Sarah was referring.

"The lady with the little girl," said Sarah. "Is that your mother?"

"Oh her?" said Tina. "Well, no...she isn't."

Nathaniel, who had been inspecting a fire hydrant, turned around and stared at Tina.

"That's...uh...my baby-sitter," said Tina hoarsely.

"Oh," said Sarah. "She's pretty. What's her name?"

"Her name?" Tina didn't know what to say next. "Her name is Jessica." Well, at least she was telling the truth. Her mother's name really was Jessica.

"Want to play sometime?" asked Sarah, looking a little sad.

"Sure," said Tina. She wondered how she was going to hide her mother from Sarah for the rest of her life.

"I have to go inside now," said Sarah. "See you on Monday."

"OK," said Tina. Thank goodness. Her

mother and Angela were still some distance away.

Nathaniel was still staring at Tina in amazement. "How are you going to get out of that one?" he asked.

Tina shrugged. She felt confused.

They all crossed the street and walked toward Broadway, which was a busy street.

"Mum!" said Tina. "Please don't sing here," she begged.

People were passing by. Tina knew they were all thinking the same thing. They were saying to themselves, "Will you just look at that crazy woman with the three children?"

"Mum, please. Everyone can hear." Tina felt she was going to cry any minute.

"Don't be silly, dear," her mother said. "I enjoy singing."

Tina and Melissa

"Were you away for the weekend?" Tina asked Melissa on Monday as they were walking home from school.

"Yes, we went to the country. It was boring."

Melissa thought everything was boring.

That summer her parents had taken her to Europe. Melissa said Europe was boring.

"Everything in Europe is boring?" Tina had asked her when she came back.

"Just about," Melissa sighed. "And the food is terrible."

And when Tina and Melissa had gone to the circus together, Tina had thought the animal act was pretty exciting. Eighteen tigers had jumped through flaming hoops. But later she had agreed with Melissa that it was all "extremely babyish."

As they walked home, Tina tried to walk like Melissa. Melissa walked like a ballet dancer. She was small and graceful. Every once in a while, she tossed back her long blonde hair, which fell over one eye. Tina admired the way Melissa wore her hair. She once told Melissa it made her look sophisticated. Melissa had been quite pleased.

Melissa tossed her hair back again.

"I've never been so bored in my entire life," she continued. "We spent the whole weekend driving around looking at antiques." She giggled. "My father says they take brand-new furniture and throw it around and hammer all over it and then try to sell it to you as a valuable old antique."

Tina giggled, too. She thought Melissa's father was funny. He told jokes all the time and Melissa always said, "DADDY!" as if she were very annoyed with him.

They walked for a while without saying anything. Then Melissa turned to Tina and said very fast, "I-can-come-to-your-house-today-if-you-want-me-to."

"Oh," said Tina. "Um...today isn't a very good day. I can't have anyone over today."

Melissa looked hurt. Tina felt bad.

"I'm being punished," said Tina.

"Really?" asked Melissa. "For what?"

Tina said as casually as she could, "Oh, my room was a mess so my mother said I couldn't have anyone over for two weeks."

The first part was true. Her room had been a mess. Her mother had yelled at her for living in a pig sty. But Tina had cleaned it up. She had cleaned it up by stuffing everything into her wardrobe. Of course her mother didn't know that. Her mother had been pleased when she saw how neat the room looked. She had never told Tina she couldn't invite anyone over.

It was Tina who had decided never to invite anyone over again. The last time Melissa had come to visit, her mother had started out by asking Melissa all kinds of silly questions, such as, "Do you have any hobbies?"

Then her mother practised singing for an hour.

Then the toilet wouldn't flush.

Then her mother screamed at Nathaniel for using her best bathing suit as a sling shot to launch rockets out the window. ("But it's in the interest of *science*," Nathaniel kept saying.)

Finally, when her mother found out that Angela had peeled a whole carrot into her furry bedroom slippers, she lost her temper and said everyone had to stay in one place and watch television for the rest of the afternoon.

"But Melissa's not allowed to watch television," Tina had whispered to her mother. Tina was mortified. How could her mother be so stupid?

When Tina and Melissa reached the corner of Tina's street, Melissa said, "Well, I'll see you tomorrow."

Tina didn't move. Then she said shyly, "Are you doing anything this afternoon?"

"What?" asked Melissa as if she hadn't heard right. "I thought you were being punished."

"I am," said Tina. "But I could go to your house."

"Well," said Melissa. She stood on the footpath twisting a piece of her blonde hair around her finger. "I guess you can."

"I'll wait outside while you ask," Tina said when they got to Melissa's house.

She sat down on the steps to wait. She saw Sarah come out of the building across the street. Sarah was carrying a long skipping rope. When she saw Tina, she began waving and calling.

"Tina, Tina!" Tina pretended not to notice her.

Sarah crossed the street. "Hi, Tina, what are you doing?"

"Oh, hi," said Tina.

Sarah looked up and down the street.

"Waiting for your baby-sitter?"

"No, she's off today," said Tina.

"Does she baby-sit every day?"

"Almost every day," said Tina. "Sometimes she sleeps overnight."

"Really?" asked Sarah. Sarah was quiet for a moment. Then she said, "Want to skip?"

"No, thanks," said Tina.

"Oh." Sarah thought for a few seconds. Then she said, "I was thinking about selling lemonade. Want to help?"

"I can't," said Tina. "I have to go to Melissa's house."

"Oh," said Sarah, looking up at Melissa's house, "I don't have to sell lemonade."

"Well, I can't really invite you in to play," Tina apologized. "Although I would if I could. I don't even know if I'm invited yet. Melissa's asking her mother."

"Oh boy," said Sarah, sitting down on the steps next to Tina. "If she says no, you could come to my house."

Sarah made Tina feel uncomfortable. She seemed so anxious to make friends.

"It's OK," sang Melissa, running down the steps. She stopped short when she saw Sarah.

"Hi, Melissa," said Sarah.

Melissa didn't say hi. She turned to Tina and said sharply, "Well, are you coming or not? My mother says it's OK."

Melissa could be very rude. Tina felt someone should say something to Sarah, so she said, "Maybe another time," and followed Melissa up the steps.

"What was that all about?" asked Melissa

when they got inside. "I didn't know you two were such big friends."

"Don't you like her?" asked Tina timidly. She knew Melissa got jealous easily.

"Are you kidding? I can't stand her. Boring! *'Melissa, want to play?' 'Melissa, want to sell lemonade?'* " Melissa gave a squeaky imitation of Sarah.

Tina looked out the window in the front hall. Sarah was still sitting on the steps looking at the ground.

The Wonderful Mrs. Glenn

In the front hall of Melissa's house there was a large oil painting with a tiny light shining down on it. It was a painting of Melissa when she was very young — maybe four years old. Her blonde hair was slightly curled and pulled back with a big bow. She was wearing an old-fashioned white pinafore and high white shoes. Melissa was watering flowers in a big garden. Tina thought the picture was the most beautiful painting she had ever seen.

"Hello, honey." Mrs. Glenn was in the kitchen. "Sit down. I'm sure you need some of my special homemade brownies."

Mrs. Glenn looked wonderful. Tina always felt excited when she saw her. Today Mrs. Glenn was wearing a white tennis dress with red rick-rack on the sleeves. A white scarf was tied around her perfect hairdo and she wore white sneakers trimmed in red. Mrs. Glenn kept in shape by jogging and playing tennis.

She was always suntanned — even in the middle of winter.

"Hello," said Tina. She tried not to stare too hard at Mrs. Glenn. "Can I call my mother to tell her where I am?"

"Certainly, darling." Mrs. Glenn ruffled Tina's short hair. Tina felt herself blushing, but she felt very happy.

The telephone was on the kitchen wall. When Tina reached her mother, her mother said she would pick her up at five.

"No," Tina said too loudly. Mrs. Glenn was watching her. "I mean that won't be necessary. I'll come home before it gets dark."

"Well, all right," her mother said.

When Tina got off the phone, she sat down at the kitchen table. Mrs. Glenn was studying her sympathetically. "I hear you're having some problems at home."

At first Tina couldn't figure out what Mrs. Glenn was talking about. Then she remembered that she had told Melissa she was being punished.

"I didn't clean my room," Tina said.

Mrs. Glenn nodded as if she understood everything. Suddenly Tina wanted to confide in her. She wanted to tell Mrs. Glenn how wonderful she was and how she wished her own mother could be just like her. But all she said was, "My mother yelled her head off."

Mrs. Glenn looked very thoughtful. Then she said, more to herself than to Tina, "Hmm, I wonder what she expects to accomplish by that."

"She yells a lot," said Tina. Tina didn't usually talk to people outside the family about her mother, but she knew Mrs. Glenn was very interested in "problems at home." Mrs. Glenn read lots of books on child psychology and had very definite ideas about raising children.

Tina never heard Mrs. Glenn raise her voice. Mrs. Glenn believed in being positive. For instance, she would never say, "Get your filthy feet off the couch." Instead, she said, "Melissa, dear, feet belong on the floor."

"Hmm," said Mrs. Glenn again. "I wonder if your mother has read the Berenstein article called, 'Pre-adolescence and Nesting Behaviour.' "

"I'm sure she hasn't," said Tina quickly. "But she said my room looked like a rat's nest."

Then Mrs. Glenn gave the most beautiful laugh. It sounded just like bells. She reached over and ruffled Tina's hair again — very gently.

"Pauvre petite," she said. Mrs. Glenn spoke French a lot. When it was time for dinner, she always said, *"Messieurs et mesdames, le dîner est servi."* It gave Tina chills of pleasure.

"I'm awfully sorry I have to go for a tennis lesson now," said Mrs. Glenn. "If you need anything, Mrs. Simon will be here." Mrs. Simon was the housekeeper who came every day.

Mrs. Glenn picked up her tennis racket. The cover was red and white and matched her tennis dress. "Now, dear, make yourself comfortable," she said to Tina. "Remember, this is your home away from home. Maybe we can have a nice long chat when I get back."

"Sure," said Tina. Melissa was poking her brownie and looking bored.

"You're so lucky," whispered Tina when they heard the door close.

"Do you think so?" asked Melissa coldly. Tina realized she was boring Melissa.

"Let's go upstairs," said Melissa.

Melissa's room was the perfect child's room. It looked like a picture in a magazine. She had a big bed with a pink organdy canopy over it and a pink bedspread. There was a window seat covered with pink organdy cushions. The room was always very neat. Mrs. Simon cleaned it every day. Melissa just had to keep her toy shelf neat.

Melissa curled herself up gracefully on the bed. "What do you want to do?" Tina looked at the toys on the shelf. Melissa had lots of toys and games, but they were all educational. Melissa was only allowed to play with toys that helped you learn.

"What about Magic with Metrics?" asked Tina.

"Nah," said Melissa.

"We could work on the Pollution Puzzle," suggested Tina.

"Ugh," said Melissa. Then she said, "I know."

"What?" asked Tina.

"We could watch television," said Melissa gleefully.

"No!" said Tina, horrified. "You're not allowed."

But Tina knew that Melissa did watch television. Melissa often stole her mother's tiny portable television and put it under her bed. Then she turned on the water in the bathtub to drown out the sound. She often lay under her pink organdy bed all afternoon watching cartoons.

Tina didn't want to be caught watching television with Melissa. What if Mrs. Glenn found them and thought it was Tina who was the bad influence. Besides, Tina didn't even like watching television.

"I just don't feel like it," said Tina.

"You're getting boring, Tina," said Melissa with a warning note in her voice.

Melissa pulled herself off the bed and walked over to the window. She sat down on the window seat.

"Will you just look at that!" said Melissa. Tina went over to the window and looked out.

Sarah was skipping with kids who looked about five or six years old. They couldn't even turn the rope. Sarah was patiently trying to show one little girl how to turn the rope without getting it all twisted up.

"I can't believe it!" Melissa tossed her hair back. "Only babies will play with her. How boring!"

Tina wandered around the room. She didn't think it was so interesting to spend the afternoon looking out the window, making fun of Sarah, but Melissa seemed very amused.

She took out the Pollution Puzzle and worked on it for a while. Then she gave up and went over to Melissa.

"Can I look in your mother's room?" she whispered.

"I don't care," said Melissa. "Now look what she's doing!" Tina looked. Sarah was giving the little kids piggyback rides, bouncing them up and down the street.

Tina went into Mr. and Mrs. Glenn's bedroom. She always loved the way it smelled — just like roses. Everything was very neat. Tina tiptoed to the wardrobe and opened the folding doors.

It was an enormous wardrobe. Mrs. Glenn's

clothes were neatly hung in rows. It was just like a doll's wardrobe. She had lots of different sports outfits and cocktail dresses — long evening gowns and matching blue jean sets.

But Tina's favourite sight were the shoes. Mrs. Glenn had about thirty pairs of shoes. They were arranged in cubbyholes all along one wall of the wardrobe. Tina sat on the floor and studied the shoes. She liked one pair of shoes best of all. They were the dark green satin party sandals. Imagine having a mother with shoes like that!

Tina tried to figure out what Mrs. Glenn would wear to the country club dance. She tried to pick the dress that went best with the green shoes.

After that, she picked an outfit for Mrs. Glenn to wear to the big annual meeting of the PTA. "It should be sensible," thought Tina, "but colourful."

The folding doors squeaked. Tina jumped. Melissa was peering in at her.

"What are you doing in there?"

Fame and Fortune

Melissa didn't wait for an answer. Her eyes were sparkling. She pulled Tina out of the wardrobe, grabbing her by both hands.

"Oh, Tina, how could we forget."

"What?" said Tina.

"Our Best-Selling Novel. We've got to work on our Best-Selling Novel."

Tina was delighted. They ran back into Melissa's room.

Melissa pulled out a pile of old magazines and paperbacks from the bottom drawer of her desk. Then she pulled out a notebook.

Tina and Melissa had started their Best-Selling Novel a few months earlier. Since they were both planning to be famous authors when they grew up, they figured they'd better have something published before they were ten. They had borrowed magazines and books from the housekeeper, Mrs. Simon, to get some idea of what grown-ups liked to read. All Mrs. Simon's books had pictures on the cover of ladies in long flowing dresses with a castle or large, mysterious house in the background. They never told Mrs. Simon why they wanted the books and magazines.

They called it their Best-Selling Novel because they hadn't picked a title yet. Tina had felt it should be mostly a mystery story, but Melissa said love stories sold more books. They both agreed that a castle in Hawaii would be a good setting for the story.

No one knew about it. Tina and Melissa wanted to surprise everyone when the book came out. The last time they had worked on their Best-Selling Novel, they had spent most of the time deciding what they would do with the millions of dollars they would make on it.

Melissa opened the notebook and read.

"Little did Lady Penelope Pembleton-Harkness know..."

That was all they had written so far. But they both knew it was awfully good.

Melissa and Tina flopped down on the white furry rug that covered the floor. They chewed on their pencils and thought very hard for a few minutes.

Then Melissa said, "Can you see everyone's face when we walk into class with the book?"

"Not to mention our picture on the back cover," added Tina.

"I was wondering what we should wear for the photograph," said Melissa.

"Oh, long black velvet dresses with black lace all over them."

"Lots of eye shadow," suggested Melissa.

After they had planned the photograph for the back cover and decided what to wear at the autographing party at school, they decided to get back to work.

"Read it again," said Melissa.

"Little did Lady Penelope Pembleton-Harkness know..."

"I've got it," shouted Melissa.

"Oh boy!" said Tina: "What?"

"...that lurking..."

"Huh?" said Tina.

"...that lurking...that lurking..."

"Oh, I get it," said Tina.

Then she read it over. "Little did Lady Penelope Pembleton-Harkness know that lurking..."

"Wow!" said Tina. "You're a genius."

"Do you think so?" asked Melissa.

Then they chewed their pencils some more.

Tina suddenly felt an idea come to her. She said very slowly, "...lurking in the shadow of the..."

"Go on! Go on!" Melissa was very excited.

"...of the...of the...OF THE PETUNIA BUSH!" Tina shouted.

"PETUNIA BUSH?" shrieked Melissa. She began to laugh. Tina was laughing too.

"Well, something *like* petunia bush."

"I know what you mean," said Melissa. "It should be something that grows around castles in Hawaii."

"Pineapples?" asked Tina. "...lurking in the shadow of the pineapple bush?"

"Not romantic enough," said Melissa. "But I just love 'lurking in the shadow.' " She said it very low and mysteriously.

Tina felt wonderful.

"I think pomegranates grow in Hawaii," Melissa said.

"What are they?" asked Tina. Melissa was *so* sophisticated.

"Oh, some kind of fruit," said Melissa.

It did sound good.

Together, they read: "Little did Lady Penelope Pembleton-Harkness know that lurking in the shadow of the pomegranate bush..."

"We haven't decided what's lurking yet," said Melissa.

"Something horrible beyond belief," said Tina.

"No, it should be her tall, dark, handsome lover," said Melissa.

"Like Mr. Smelt." Tina giggled. Mr. Smelt was their headmaster.

"No!" shrieked Melissa. "He's horrible beyond belief."

"OK," said Tina. "...lurking in the shadow of the pomegranate bush was something horrible beyond belief, her headmaster, Mr. Smelt..."

"...picking his nose..." added Melissa.

Tina burst out laughing. They were both laughing so hard, they were rolling on the floor hugging each other.

"I've seen him pick his nose," said Melissa, gasping for air.

"Me too," howled Tina.

Tina had forgotten all about Sarah. She forgot how mean Melissa could be. Melissa was more fun than anyone she knew. They had such a good time together.

When they finally stopped laughing, Melissa said, "We don't have to decide what's lurking yet."

"No," sighed Tina. "We've done enough for today." She read it one more time. "It's so good."

"Maybe we should show it to somebody," said Melissa suddenly.

"What?" Tina was surprised. "But it's supposed to be a secret."

"But we need an opinion," said Melissa.

"Maybe we should show it to Mrs. Simon. She reads things like this all the time."

"She might tell your mother."

"True," said Melissa thoughtfully.

Melissa wandered over to the window.

"We could show it to *her*!" she said.

"You mean Sarah?" Tina could never figure Melissa out.

"Sure. Why not?" said Melissa. "We ought to show it to *somebody*. But we should type it first. It'll look more professional."

Tina followed Melissa into the room Mrs. Glenn used for an office. She watched her type.

Then they both ran out the front door and down the steps.

"Sarah! Sarah!" they both shouted.

Sarah was sitting on the kerb with her skipping rope. She looked up.

To her surprise she saw Tina and Melissa coming across the street waving at her.

"Sarah! Sarah! We need your help..."

"...desperately..." added Melissa, smiling at her.

"You do?" asked Sarah, staring at them. She looked stunned.

"C'mon!" Melissa grabbed her hand and dragged her across the street to her front steps.

"Now sit down," said Melissa. Sarah looked at Tina as if to ask if this were all a joke.

"It's all right," said Tina gently. "Sit down."

"You see..." Melissa began, "...we're working on a Best-Selling Novel..."

"...and we need someone to read it so far and tell us what they think," Tina said.

"Really?" asked Sarah, looking from one to the other.

"It's top secret," said Melissa. "You've got to promise not to tell anyone — until it's on the shelf at your local neighbourhood bookshop."

"Oh, I won't tell anyone," said Sarah. "Besides, I don't know anyone to tell."

"You'll get a free autographed copy, of course," said Tina.

"Really?"

Melissa pulled out the typewritten piece of paper. Then Melissa and Tina looked away while Sarah read it. They didn't want to make her nervous.

"Gosh," said Sarah when she finished. (It didn't take her very long.) "It's just like a real grown-up book." Tina and Melissa beamed. "And it's so exciting so far."

"Oh, we have a little work to do on it still," said Melissa modestly.

"What's going to happen?" asked Sarah.

"We're not exactly sure," said Tina. "We've still got to put on the finishing touches."

"And write the story," Melissa admitted. "It all takes place in a castle in Hawaii."

"Oooh," said Sarah. "That gives me shivers all over." She gave a big sigh. "I can just hear the waves pounding against the cliffs."

"Wait a minute!" said Melissa. "Hold everything!" She turned to Sarah and said sharply, "What did you say?"

Sarah shrugged. She looked a little scared. "I just said, 'I can just hear the waves pounding against the cliffs.'"

"Not bad," said Melissa thoughtfully. She looked at Tina. "We should write that."

For just a second Tina felt a sharp twinge of jealousy. She had been feeling so happy that Melissa was being friendly to Sarah. She looked at Melissa and Sarah, who were both watching her. For a moment she wished she were Sarah and lived right across the street from Melissa.

"I'm not sure I like it," she said slowly. Then she felt very mean. "Yes, I guess I do," she said. "C'mon, Melissa, let's go upstairs and write it down." She wanted to get away from Sarah.

"Well, bye," said Melissa to Sarah. "Thanks for your help."

"Bye." Sarah was grinning. "I can't wait to read it when it's all finished."

When it was time to go, Tina went down to the kitchen to say good-bye to Mrs. Glenn, who had returned from her tennis lesson. Now Mrs. Glenn was wearing a flowered dress that fitted her perfectly and a matching flowered apron. She was wearing a hairnet — she always wore a hairnet in the kitchen — and was rolling out dough for a quiche. Tina had once tasted Mrs. Glenn's quiche. It turned out to be cheese pie. Tina thought it was delicious.

The kitchen smelled wonderful. Mrs. Glenn didn't believe in packaged foods; she made everything from scratch — biscuits, bread, marmalade.

"You're more than welcome to stay for dinner," said Mrs. Glenn, looking very beautiful, but very motherly at the same time.

"Oh, thank you," said Tina. "But I told my mother I'd be home before dark."

"Well, anytime you need someone to talk to, I'll be here." She smiled at Tina.

Tina skipped down the steps of Melissa's house.

"Just like my fairy godmother," she thought.

A Problem for Science

"Hi, dear," Tina's mother said when Tina got home.

Her mother was in the hall packing Angela into the backseat of her bicycle. She was wearing an old plaid skirt, a striped blouse, and her blue-flowered scarf on her head.

"I forgot to buy a few things at the supermarket. I'll be right back..."

"... in a jifferly..." Angela said, and stuck her thumb into her mouth.

"Oh, Christina," her mother said as she wheeled the bicycle toward the door. "Your room!"

"Huh?" asked Tina. She was still in a daze from her visit to Mrs. Glenn.

"I want it cleaned up by the time I get back."

"It'll only get messy again," mumbled Tina.

Tina helped them to the lift.

Why did her mother have to ride around on

a bicycle? It was so undignified. And why did she always forget something and have to go out at the last minute?

Tina's mother never knew what they were having to eat until half an hour before dinner. Then she would throw something together. It usually tasted good, but that wasn't the point. Why couldn't she be organized like Mrs. Glenn?

As soon as the lift door closed, Tina heard her mother begin to sing.

"Un' bel di vedremo..." Her mother always sang the same song in the lift. It was an aria from *Madame Butterfly* and Tina hated it.

She ran back into her apartment and slammed the door. She stuck her fingers in her ears. She was sure everyone in the whole building could hear her mother's voice.

As she was cleaning up her room, she noticed a note on top of a pile of papers lying on her desk. It was a note about Parent-Teacher Conference Night. She was supposed to give it to her mother to sign.

Tina sat down on her bed and studied the note. Parent-Teacher Conference Night wasn't until next week, but the note was supposed to be signed and returned this Friday. Tina wanted to tear it up.

She couldn't do that, so she folded it neatly and stuck it into the pocket of her school bag. She counted on her fingers. She had three days to figure out what to do with that note.

Tina lay on her bed and stared at the ceiling. What was she going to do about her mother?

Finally she got up and went to Nathaniel's room. His door was closed. Tina knocked softly.

"What?" called Nathaniel.

Tina peered in. "Can I come in?" she asked. "I've got to talk to you."

"About what?" Nathaniel didn't even look up. He was sitting at a table, carefully packing live cockroaches into paper cups filled

with ice. He was working on his latest experiment.

"About mother, of course," said Tina.

"Oh, her." Nathaniel and Tina agreed on one thing: their mother and how much she embarrassed them.

"You'll have to wait," said Nathaniel. "I have to get these in the freezer before the ice melts."

Tina sat on the bed and watched Nathaniel pack cockroaches in ice.

This was to be a long-range experiment. Nathaniel's plan was to freeze the cockroaches alive and in fifty years he would take them out of the freezer and bring them back to life.

When Tina had first heard about the

experiment, she had said, "But you'll be sixty-one years old then. We might not even live here."

Today she asked, "What's the point, anyway? Why do you want to put cockroaches in animated suspension?"

"Suspended animation," Nathaniel corrected her. "You see, people can be put into deep freeze when they have a rare disease. Someday scientists will discover a cure for that disease and then they will bring the people back to life and cure them. Very simple."

"These cockroaches don't have a rare disease," argued Tina. "I just don't get it."

Nathaniel sealed the paper cup. Then he looked at Tina as if he felt very sorry for her.

"Don't you understand? This is pure science. Pure science doesn't have to have a point."

He took the cup to the kitchen and returned a minute later.

"Besides, I have fifty years to think about it," he said, sitting down again at the table he called his scientific laboratory.

"Now," he said. "What's the problem and can we use my computer to solve it?"

"Oh, no," said Tina. She didn't want to get involved with the computer Nathaniel had built. It was impressive-looking with flashing lights and buttons, but all the information had to be fed into it by punching holes in different places on long tapes. The holes meant "Yes," "No," and "Maybe," depending on where you put them. It wasn't a real computer and Tina thought it would be easier just to make a list.

Tina and Nathaniel had used it to figure out what would be an ideal pet for their family. When they finally finished feeding the computer the information, Nathaniel said the computer said that a chimpanzee would be the perfect pet. But their mother said a city apartment was no place for an ape, or even a cat.

"We have to do something about Mum's behaviour," moaned Tina. "You know — the things she does, the things she talks about, the way she acts in public..." Tina shuddered. "Like what happened on the bus last Saturday."

Nathaniel blushed. "That was awful."

"Her singing," added Tina.

"Ugh," said Nathaniel. "But grown-up behaviour is a very difficult problem for science."

Tina knew that Nathaniel was only

interested in problems that could be worked on scientifically.

"Let me think," said Nathaniel, and he began pacing up and down the room. "There was something I read..."

Tina waited.

Suddenly Nathaniel stopped pacing. "That's it!" He snapped his fingers. "The article I read in *Gee Whiz*."

Gee Whiz was a science magazine for kids. Nathaniel got it every month.

"It's all about behaviour modification."

"Behaviour modification?" asked Tina.

"Yeah, it's sort of reprogramming — changing behaviour. It works on rats all the time."

"Mum's not a rat," said Tina.

"Doesn't matter," said Nathaniel. "I'm sure it works on people, too. In fact, I know it does. They use it on people — criminals and people like that — all the time."

"Well?" asked Tina. She watched Nathaniel tear through a pile of old science magazines. He was very excited. Tina was beginning to feel excited herself.

"It works on flatworms, too," Nathaniel was saying. "In fact, after they train one flatworm to behave and find its way through a maze, they mash him up and feed him to another flatworm. The second flatworm learns how to get through the maze much faster than the first one."

"But Mum's not a flatworm." Tina was almost shouting by now.

Just then they heard their mother's voice. She was back.

"*La donna e mobile...*" she sang.

"I've got to find that article," said Nathaniel. "Believe me, behaviour modification will work."

At dinner that night, Tina listened to her mother tell how she had tried to call the bus company all day to complain about the rude driver on Saturday.

"If only I had thought to get his number," her mother was saying.

Tina looked at her father. He was listening politely to her mother. Tina's father played the cello in the city orchestra, and Tina was proud of him. But she wondered if she and Nathaniel should use some behaviour modification on him, too.

The only really embarrassing thing about her father was his clothes.

When he got home from rehearsals, he changed into an old suit. He didn't change into sports clothes like other fathers. He didn't even wear blue jeans and an old plaid shirt. He wore old dress shirts and suits with patches on the sleeves. He never looked relaxed.

Tina decided her mother was a more serious problem. Once they cured her, they could do just about anything.

Tina dragged her fork through her mashed potatoes.

She found herself wondering what would happen if they mashed up Mrs. Glenn and fed her to their mother. "Maybe she would improve like the flatworms," she thought.

"What are you giggling about, Tina?" her father asked, smiling at her.

"Oh, nothing," said Tina. She smiled at Nathaniel.

The Embarrassing Lunch

On Friday morning Tina just couldn't bring herself to show her mother the note about the Parent-Teacher Conference.

Last year Parent-Teacher Conference Night had been horrible. Her mother kept asking her teacher all kinds of silly questions. She didn't ask a single question about schoolwork. She asked if all the children got along with each other. She asked if they had enough fresh air. She asked if the school custodians kept the bathrooms clean.

Then she told Tina's teacher how much she had hated school herself. What a horrible teacher she herself had had. She took longer than any other parent. Tina's father just sat there without saying a word.

Then, in the hall, her mother started talking to Melissa's mother about how well the girls got along. Mrs. Glenn just smiled and nodded and, at the same time, waved to other mothers who passed by.

"She's just being polite," thought Tina. She was terribly embarrassed. Mrs. Glenn looked so grown-up and dignified next to Tina's mother, who was wearing her blue-flowered scarf around her head and flat sandals that looked like bedroom slippers.

Tina sat at the breakfast table and watched her mother making lunch for school. Her mother was putting leftover meat and salad into little plastic bowls with lids. That's what Tina and Nathaniel had to take to school every day for lunch. It was such an embarrassing lunch. If Tina sat with someone she didn't know very well, she often didn't even open her lunchbox. She wished she could have plain sandwiches like everyone else.

Tina's mother was tugging at the box of frozen waffles in the freezer.

"A lady called last night," she said.

"Who?" asked Tina.

"Mrs. Walker. Sarah's mother."

Tina choked on her orange juice. Nathaniel was watching her.

"I don't know Sarah, do I?" Her mother took some waffles out of the package and put the rest back into the freezer. "What are all these paper cups doing in the freezer?"

"Leave them," said Nathaniel. "They are a very important experiment."

"Anyway," their mother continued, putting the paper cups back. "She wanted to know if she could have the phone number for my baby-sitter. Sarah told her we have a nice baby-sitter, named Jessica."

Tina was holding her breath. Her mother popped the waffles in the toaster.

"So I said I had only one baby-sitter, but her name was Jennifer, so I gave her Jennifer's phone number."

Tina let out her breath with relief. Jennifer and Jessica were very similar names. But what would Sarah think when the wrong baby-sitter arrived? Tina thought she could figure out some way to explain that to Sarah.

But her mother was still talking.

"Then Mrs. Walker called back. Jennifer couldn't baby-sit and Mrs. Walker needed someone desperately for this afternoon. She has a dance class and will be home late. So I said Sarah would be welcome to come here."

"No!" shouted Tina. This was the worst thing that could have happened.

"What's the matter?" Her mother looked puzzled. "Don't you like her?"

Tina liked Sarah a lot. "No, I don't," she said.

"Well, one afternoon won't kill you." Her mother smiled. "Besides, it's about time you had someone over to visit. You don't even invite Melissa here anymore. And you always go there."

Tina felt like shouting, "Well, that's your fault."

Tina's mother left the kitchen to get Angela up. Nathaniel leaned over and whispered, "Electric shocks."

"Huh?" said Tina, staring at Nathaniel.

"Electric shocks. That's how behaviour modification works. You give them electric shocks when they do something you don't want them to do."

"Oh, great," said Tina. "You and your dumb science." Nathaniel looked so hurt, she said, "I'm sorry, Nathaniel. I didn't mean it, but *what am I going to do about Sarah?*"

"I'm afraid…" said Nathaniel. "That's not a problem for science."

Tina felt so sick she couldn't eat any of her waffle.

Tina walked slowly to school, trying to figure out what she was going to do.

Sarah was waiting on the school steps. Her brown hair was parted in the middle and pulled back with two pink slides in the shape of elephants. Her face was shining. She looked happy and excited.

"Did your mother tell you? I'm coming to your house today."

"I know," said Tina.

"Jennifer couldn't baby-sit," said Sarah. "She was busy." She looked at Tina. "I thought you said her name was Jessica."

Tina could have told the truth right then. All she had to do was to say she had lied. She looked at Sarah. Sarah seemed to trust her so much.

"The reason she was busy is because she is baby-sitting for us," said Tina.

"Oh, boy," said Sarah. "The same one? She looks so nice. Well, what is her name — Jennifer or Jessica?"

"Well," said Tina slowly. "I call her Jessica.

Jennifer is her real name, but she likes Jessica better."

"I don't blame her," said Sarah. Tina was surprised. Maybe she could get away with it. If she could just get to Nathaniel and warn him. He would understand.

Then she remembered that Nathaniel had his football game on Friday. She wouldn't even have to worry about him.

"My little sister Angela calls Jessica 'Mummy,'" said Tina. "My little sister calls everyone 'Mummy.'"

"How cute," said Sarah. "I wish I had a little sister." They walked into class together and hung their sweaters in the coat cupboard.

Melissa was already in her seat.

"Hi," said Sarah to Melissa. "Guess what. I'm going to Tina's house today."

Melissa stared at Sarah. Then she turned to Tina with a shocked expression on her face. Slowly, she turned her back on Tina and Sarah and began piling her workbooks very carefully on her desk.

"Everyone in your seat," called their teacher. Mrs. Turner rapped on her desk. "Then pass in your notices about the Parent-Teacher Conference."

Tina didn't know what to do. She pulled her

notice out of the pocket of her school bag. Then she looked around.

Quickly, she wrote at the bottom:

"Cannot come. Have another apointment.
                    Sincerely,
                    Mrs. Richard Steele"

She hoped it looked all right. She had taught herself to write cursive when she was only six. She had practised by writing her mother's name, just the way her mother wrote it.

She folded the note and passed it to the front of the class. Mrs. Turner didn't even look at them.

Tina couldn't believe she had told so many lies in such a short time. She didn't usually tell lies. The funny thing was that lying seemed to get easier and easier.

"I lie well," she thought.

Halfway through the morning, Tina felt something hit her leg. It was a note from Melissa:

"How come you invited Sarah to your house and you never invite me?"

Tina read it over. She never realized just how much she had been hurting Melissa's feelings. All she ever thought about was how much her mother embarrassed her.

Tina wrote at the bottom of the note, "*My mother made me invite her.*"

Then she scribbled it out. She couldn't say that! Melissa thought her mother wouldn't allow her to have anyone over. Tina sat and thought. She turned the piece of paper over and began to write again:

"*My baby-sitter will only allow me to have one guest....*" No, that was no good. Melissa didn't even know she was supposed to have a baby-sitter. That was the story she told Sarah. Tina felt very confused. She tried again.

"*My mother made me invite Sarah over as a punishment....*"

Tina was beginning to wonder if she ought to keep a diary of all the lies she had told recently so she could keep them straight. She crumpled up the note in her hand.

She shouldn't have done that. Melissa was watching her in disbelief. Then Melissa's expression changed. She looked at Tina as if she hated her.

Tina quickly took another piece of paper and wrote Melissa another note.

"*I will explain everything at lunch.*"

She slipped it quickly onto Melissa's desk.

At lunchtime Tina saved a place at her table for Melissa. She waited, wondering how she was going to explain anything at all. She was almost relieved when she saw Melissa sit down at a table far away.

Sarah came and sat down next to Tina. Tina closed her lunchbox in a hurry. She wasn't ashamed of eating when she sat with Melissa; Melissa was used to seeing the weird lunches Tina brought to school every day, but Sarah was new.

Tina and Sarah sat for a few minutes. Sarah asked Tina some questions about the Best-Selling Novel, but she didn't open her lunchbox either. She seemed nervous.

"Well," Sarah finally said. "I guess we'd better eat."

"I guess so," said Tina. "But I don't feel very hungry today." She *was* hungry. In fact, she was starving. She wished she had been able to eat the waffle for breakfast.

Sarah finally gave in. She opened her lunchbox. She took out a piece of cold pizza and began to eat it. Tina watched in amazement as Sarah opened a little plastic container and ate something that looked like cold spinach with a fork.

Tina opened her own lunchbox and began to eat. She was beginning to feel better.

Sarah's lunch was worse than hers.

During recess Tina went to the coin phone and called her mother.

"What's the matter?" Her mother sounded worried.

"Oh, nothing, but Mum..." Tina didn't want to hurt her mother's feelings. "Mum, when Sarah comes over, could you leave us alone?"

"Well, I wasn't planning to play with you." Her mother sounded hurt.

"Oh, Mum, you know what I mean. Don't ask her all kinds of questions — you know. Just don't say anything."

"I baked you some cupcakes," her mother said in a very small voice.

"Could you just leave them on the table?" Tina was beginning to feel like a monster.

"Well, I have plenty to do anyway."

"Another thing, Mum." Tina paused. "Do you mind if I call you Jessica — just for today. It sounds...um...more grown-up."

Her mother didn't answer. Then she said, "Tina, are you sure everything is all right? You've been acting strangely lately."

"Oh sure, Mum."

There was a silence at the other end. Then her mother said, "Is that all you called about?"

"Yes," said Tina. "Well, bye." She hung up.

Everything was under control. Tina was quite sure she hadn't forgotten a thing.

A Date with Sarah

Tina's mother opened the door and smiled at Sarah.

"Hi, Jessica," said Sarah shyly. Tina's mother stopped smiling. She wasn't used to children calling her by her first name — not the first time they met, anyway.

Angela ran to the door and hugged Tina. Then she hid behind Tina and peered out at Sarah.

"Cupcakes and milk are on the kitchen table," said Tina's mother. Tina thought she was trying too hard to sound cheerful. "I've got plenty of work to do." She gave Tina a look which seemed to say, "Don't worry — I won't bother you."

Angela followed Sarah and Tina into the kitchen.

"New shoes," Angela said to Sarah.

Tina almost called out, "Mum..." Then she caught herself. "Oh, Jessica..." she called.

"Jessica, could you make Angela go somewhere else?"

"No, no," said Sarah. "Let her stay — please."

"We don't want her around. She gets to be a pest."

"Oh, please," begged Sarah. "She's so cute."

Angela had got over her shyness and was holding Sarah's hand.

"Is this her seat?" Sarah put Angela's little seat on top of a chair and helped Angela climb up.

"I want a cupcake," said Angela. She began pounding on the table.

Tina looked at the cupcakes on the table. They were beautiful. There were six cupcakes in three different colours: pink with red roses on top; chocolate with yellow roses and vanilla cupcakes with pink *and* yellow roses. Her mother had gone to so much trouble. Tina felt sad.

"Mummy made them," said Angela proudly.

"You mean Jessica made them," Tina said quickly. "She calls everyone 'Mummy,'" Tina told Sarah again in case she forgot. Tina tried to laugh, but her face felt stiff. "She'll probably call you 'Mummy' too."

Angela got mad. "Not Mummy. That's Sarah."

Tina decided to ignore this. She waited for Sarah to choose a cupcake. Sarah took a pink one and Tina picked a chocolate one.

"Umm...delicious," said Sarah when she had finished. "You know what?"

"What?" asked Tina.

"This is the first time I've been to anyone's house since I moved in."

"Oh," said Tina. She felt glad that Sarah had come to visit even if the situation was rather difficult to handle.

Angela was already eating her third cupcake; all she ate was the icing on each one.

"Can you come over every day?" Angela asked Sarah. Then she reached for the last cupcake. Tina grabbed her hand.

"No, Angela!"

The afternoon passed quickly. Tina's mother went to take a nap.

"Does Jessica always take a nap on your mother's bed?" whispered Sarah as they tiptoed past her mother's bedroom.

"Oh, Mum doesn't mind."

That was the only time things got tricky. Sarah was very easy to please. When Tina took Sarah into her room, she suddenly realized that all her toys were piled at the bottom of her wardrobe. So she suggested that they play in Angela's room and put on plays for Angela. They could use stuffed animals as actors and actresses.

"What fun!" said Sarah.

Angela thought it was fun too. She was a good audience.

Everyone was surprised when Tina's mother knocked on Angela's door and called, "It's almost five-thirty. Sarah's got to go home now."

Sarah found her sweater and schoolbooks.

"Oh, Jessica," Sarah said to Tina's mother at the door. "I had such a good time."

"I'll walk you home," said Tina.

They were all standing in front of the door when a key turned in the lock.

Tina watched in horror. Two seconds later, her father walked in.

"Home early, dear," he said, kissing Tina's mother right on the lips.

Sarah stared at them.

"This is Tina's friend, Sarah," said Tina's

mother, hugging her father. "They entertained Angela all afternoon."

"Hi, Sarah," her father said. "Pleased to meet you."

As Tina walked Sarah to the lift, she thought of whispering that it was Jessica's boyfriend, but Sarah looked so confused, Tina gave up trying.

"I — I think I can get home by myself," said Sarah. She got into the lift and looked up at the ceiling until the door closed.

A Terrible Dream

Tina had trouble going to sleep that night. She kept trying to think up ways to explain to Sarah about her mother.

First she thought of stories such as: "Jessica is really my mother's twin sister who is visiting..." or "I had to tell you she wasn't my mother because my mother is an undercover agent and her identity must be kept a secret..."

The stories got too complicated. Tina tried to think of a way of just telling Sarah she had lied. She kept thinking of the expression on Sarah's face when she was in the lift and stared at the ceiling without even looking back at Tina.

Finally she fell asleep.

She dreamed she was walking along the beach. She was looking for something that had been lost, but she didn't even know what it was.

Suddenly a big shadow passed over her.

Following behind her was an enormous grizzly bear. Tina began to run as fast as she could. The bear started to run too.

He chased her along the beach. The beach was crowded with people on blankets and in deck chairs.

Children were making sand castles and families were pulling sandwiches out of picnic baskets.

Tina shouted "Help!" but no one looked up. No one seemed to be disturbed that a grizzly bear was chasing Tina around the beach.

At last she saw her mother. Her mother was sitting in a deck chair, wearing her blue-flowered scarf around her head. She was reading a book.

Tina ran as fast as she could. The bear was still puffing and grunting behind her. Tina jumped up into her mother's lap.

"Safe." Tina was hugging her mother hard.

Suddenly she felt her mother become furry. Her mother got furrier and furrier.

Tina suddenly realized her mother had turned into a grizzly bear — a bear wearing a blue-flowered scarf around its head...

Tina woke up from the dream. She was shaking all over. When she saw her mother sitting at the end of the bed, she shrieked and crawled under the covers.

"Tina, Tina." Her mother was shaking her. "Come out. I've got to talk to you."

Tina pulled the covers down a little and peered out. It was morning, but it was too early for school. Then Tina realized it was Saturday. She looked at her mother. Her mother looked worried. Tina was frightened. There was something the matter.

"Tina, I've got to talk to you. I received a call last night..."

"From Sarah's mother?" That was all Tina could think of.

"No, it was from your teacher, Mrs. Turner. She thinks you signed my name on a note about the Parent-Teacher Conference next week. She says you pretended I couldn't come. I had to say I didn't know anything about it."

"Oh?" said Tina, trying to look surprised.

She felt sick. She had been so busy lying to Sarah, she had forgotten all about the note.

"Tina, that's serious. That's forgery. Signing someone else's name is called forgery, and forgery is a criminal offence."

Her mother looked so upset, Tina knew it would make it worse if she said she didn't do it.

"I didn't want you to go," she said in a low voice. "Will I go to gaol?"

"Don't be silly," her mother said. "Why didn't you want me to go to the conference?"

Tina shrugged. She didn't know where to start. "I get embarrassed," was all she said.

Then she thought how embarrassed her mother must have been when Mrs. Turner called. She thought how embarrassed she would be if her child was caught forging a note. She felt very sorry for her mother having a kid like her.

"Did you say you'd go?" Tina couldn't help asking.

"Of course," her mother said. "Mrs. Turner wanted to know if I thought it would help if you had a little talk with the headmaster, Mr. Smelt, on Monday."

"Oh, no!"

"That's what I said. I told her I'd talk to you myself."

"Have you talked to me?" asked Tina.

"Well, I don't know." Her mother looked down. "It's so serious — writing someone else's name. I didn't even tell your father."

They both sat for a while without saying anything. Then Tina reached out and grabbed her mother's hand. "I'm sorry, Mum."

To her surprise, her mother giggled. "You spelled appointment wrong. It has two p's."

Tina crawled into her mother's lap and just stayed there for a while. Her mother rubbed her back and sang softly.

It didn't sound so bad.

The Whole Truth

That weekend Tina made up her mind. She was never going to tell another lie. She was going to tell Sarah the whole truth.

On Monday morning, she got dressed in a hurry and gobbled her breakfast. She wanted to get going while she still felt brave.

Tina sat on the school steps waiting for Sarah. She rehearsed what she was going to say.

"Hi, Tina. Waiting for Melissa?" Linda, the class nosy-body, sat down next to Tina.

"No," said Tina. She moved away a little.

"How come?" asked Linda. "Aren't you two friends anymore?" Tina wondered if telling the truth included telling people like Linda the whole truth. Did Linda really count?

Then she saw Sarah coming. She stood up. Sarah wasn't alone. She was walking with another girl.

Tina didn't recognize the other girl right away. As they got closer, Tina realized it was Melissa. But Melissa looked different. Her hair was parted in the middle and pulled back with two slides — just like Sarah's. When they got even closer, Tina saw they were both wearing the same pink elephant slides.

Tina turned away quickly and hurried up the school steps. Linda followed her. By the time they reached the top, Linda was panting. She kept nudging Tina in the arm.

"You had a fight, didn't you?" said Linda, giving Tina a very hard nudge. Tina turned around and looked at Linda's pink, chubby face. "Leave me alone," she muttered.

Tina sat in class trying to pay attention to the lesson. She kept telling herself, "They probably bumped into each other. It's only natural. After all, they live right across the street from each other."

But every time she caught sight of the identical pink elephant slides, she got a lump in her throat.

When Tina reached school the next day, Sarah was already there. She and Melissa were sitting on the school steps wearing their pink elephant slides. They seemed to be having a private conversation.

Tina never got a chance to talk to Sarah all that week. Sarah and Melissa were always together. On Friday afternoon, Tina decided to call Sarah on the telephone.

Her heart was thumping as she dialled Sarah's number. A lady answered the phone.

"Hello?"

"May I please talk to Sarah?"

"I'm sorry, she's not here."

"Oh," said Tina. "I just wanted the homework assignment." She hoped the lady, who was probably Sarah's mother, didn't know that they never got homework on Fridays.

"Well," said the lady. "She's at Melissa's house if you want to try there."

"No, it's OK," said Tina. And she hung up.

Tina sat in the chair staring at the phone.

When her mother came into the living room, she quickly picked up a magazine.

"Everything all right?"

"Just fine," said Tina as brightly as she could. Her mother came over and gave her a little hug.

Tina watched her mother leave the room. She wondered if right now — right this very minute — Mrs. Glenn was feeding Sarah homemade brownies. She wondered if Melissa and Sarah were sitting together on Melissa's pink organdy bed working on the Pollution Puzzle. She thought about them sitting together on the school steps and wondered what they had been talking about.

Then she had a horrible thought. What if Sarah told Melissa the whole story of Tina and the baby-sitter mix-up!

Another picture came to Tina's mind. It was a picture of Sarah lying on Melissa's white furry rug, leaning on her elbows, her chin propped up in her hands. Sarah was twirling her legs around in the air lazily.

"She has no right to be there!" Tina thought.

Sarah and her silly pink elephant slides... Sarah and her big "I'm-just-a-new-girl" act...She had probably been planning to steal Melissa from Tina all along.

The more Tina thought about it, the more she was sure that Sarah *had* told Melissa the whole story. They were probably laughing their heads off right now.

"Who cares?" she whispered aloud. Tina went to the bathroom and looked at herself in the mirror. She wanted to see if she looked as if she really didn't care.

Mothers Anonymous

That night at the Parent-Teacher Conference, Tina saw Sarah's mother for the first time. To her surprise, Sarah's mother dressed very much the way Tina's mother did — at least the way Tina's mother usually did.

But tonight Tina's mother wasn't dressed the way she usually was. She was wearing a suit, black patent leather high heels, and stockings. Her hair was much neater than usual. Tina suspected her mother had dressed that way just for her. Her mother wanted her to be proud of her instead of embarrassed. The idea of her mother going out of her way like that made Tina uncomfortable.

Tina's father wore his best suit. Tina thought it looked old-fashioned. The other fathers wore sport shirts.

Even though Tina hadn't said a word to Sarah and Melissa for almost a week, she went and stood next to them. She didn't want her mother and father to think she didn't have any friends.

Melissa treated her as if she weren't even there; she kept whispering to Sarah and turning her back on Tina. So Tina edged closer to make it look like she was still part of their little group. She pretended to be listening and taking part in the conversation.

Out of the corner of her eye, she saw her mother talking to Mrs. Glenn. Her father was wandering around the classroom, looking at the pictures on the bulletin board and the pet hamsters in their cages. He caught Tina's eye and smiled. Tina turned around quickly and moved a little closer to Sarah and Melissa.

"Oh, Melissa…" she burst out. She had to say something. Melissa stopped talking to Sarah and stared at Tina as if she thought Tina was a very rude person.

"I…er…thought of a good title for the Best-Selling Novel."

For a second Tina thought she saw a flicker of interest in Melissa's eyes.

"Oh, what?" asked Sarah. She was smiling at Tina.

Tina thought fast. "The Revenge of Lady

Penelope Pembleton-Harkness," she said. It wasn't bad, she thought.

No one said anything. Then Melissa said slowly, "Oh, by the way, we really have to change her name. It just won't do."

"Oh?" said Tina. She was shocked. She had spent hours thinking up the perfect name for Lady Penelope.

"Sarah was saying that people with double names usually have one short one and one long one — like Pembleton-Hart."

Sarah looked away. She began fumbling with one of her slides — opening it and closing it. "It was just a suggestion," she said in a low voice.

"Well, I agree with it," said Melissa.

"I guess it doesn't matter," said Tina, but she wanted to cry. She would have moved away right then, but her father was still watching her.

"No, it doesn't matter at all," said Melissa. "I'm beginning to find the whole thing pretty boring, anyway." And she turned her back on Tina.

Tina thought she had got through the evening pretty well — especially when her mother said to her afterward, "You certainly do have two very nice little friends."

They were walking home. Tina was in the middle. Her father had his hand on her neck and he kept squeezing it almost as if he were feeling sorry for her. Tina wondered if he had noticed anything. Her father didn't get fooled easily.

More than anything, Tina wanted her parents to think everything was all right.

Her mother was having a hard time walking. She wasn't used to high heels.

"Mum," said Tina. "What were you and Melissa's mother talking about?"

"Oh, it was the strangest conversation. She kept telling me about some therapy group called 'Mothers Anonymous.' It's supposed to help you get along with your children. For some reason she thought I would be interested in joining it."

Tina was sorry she had asked.

Emerald Green / Turquoise Blue

Sarah and Melissa were writing exactly alike. When their compositions were put up on the bulletin board, you couldn't tell them apart — unless you looked at the names. They wrote very small and made their "r's" with loops in them, like this: $\mathcal{r}$. Instead of regular "e's", their "e's" looked like this: $\mathcal{E}$. And their "i's" made Tina the most upset. They always made big circles over them, instead of dots: $\overset{\circ}{\iota}$. It drove Tina crazy.

The teacher sometimes said, "Write a little bigger, Sarah" and "Write bigger, Melissa; it's hard to read." But Tina didn't think it was fair that Mrs. Turner was letting them get away with their $\mathcal{r}$'s, their $\mathcal{E}$'s, and, especially, their $\overset{\circ}{\iota}$'s.

The next week Melissa and Sarah were using ball-point pens with the same colour ink — not plain old blue ink like everyone else, but "emerald green."

The next week they were both writing in turquoise ink. Then it was purple. Mrs. Turner wasn't pleased about it, but she said she supposed it was all right, as long as it wasn't red ink. Tina thought Mrs. Turner was letting them get away with murder.

And Tina thought someone should report Melissa to the teacher when she started signing her name Melissa J. Glenn. Sarah always wrote her name Sarah J. Walker, but Sarah's middle name was Jane. Melissa didn't have a middle name; Tina knew that for sure.

Tina was miserable. And her curiosity made her even more miserable. Every day she called Melissa or Sarah's house to see where they were playing that day. If Sarah or Melissa answered, she hung up immediately. If a grown-up answered, she often disguised her voice.

Tina didn't want her mother to know anything was wrong. Sometimes she told her mother she was going to Melissa's house, but she spent those afternoons in the public library doing her homework.

She became an expert eavesdropper. Her hearing became so good she could pick out a conversation between Sarah and Melissa — no matter where they were. In the lunchroom. In the gymnasium. Even in the playground.

Once she heard them talking about what they would wear for Halloween. They were going to be dressed exactly alike — like two little rag dolls.

Before Halloween came, they were discussing the Christmas holidays. Sarah might be able to visit Melissa's house in the country.

And Tina could hardly believe her ears when she heard them deciding who they would send Valentines to. That was on October 26th.

That was when Tina realized there would never be anything for her to look forward to again.

The Halloween Witch

On the day before Halloween, Tina's mother bit into a breakfast roll and lost the cap on her front tooth.

Tina nearly died. She couldn't even look her mother in the face.

"Get it fixed right away!" she pleaded.

"Well, I'll try, but I don't know if the dentist can see me today."

"Mum!" said Tina.

"It doesn't hurt," her mother said. "It's only a cap."

When Tina got home from school, her mother's tooth was still missing.

"The dentist can't see me until tomorrow," she said when she saw Tina's horrified look.

"Can't you call him again?" asked Tina desperately. "You look like a witch."

"Oh, well," her mother said. "Tomorrow's Halloween."

Tina didn't think her mother was being the least bit funny. She couldn't understand how her mother could treat a missing tooth so lightly. Tina secretly thought her mother looked worse than a witch. She looked like those beggar women who went around with lots of shopping bags.

The house was very quiet. Nathaniel was at football practice and Angela was visiting the little girl who lived downstairs. Tina went to try on her last year's Halloween costume — a dog outfit with black and white spotted ears. She took it off and folded it away in her bureau drawer. She didn't even want to go "trick-or-treating." If she couldn't be a little rag doll like Melissa and Sarah, she'd just as soon stay home.

Her mother came into her room wearing a coat. "Yikes," said Tina. She got a shock every time her mother opened her mouth.

"C'mon, Tina, I've got to get some groceries."

"What?" shouted Tina. "You can't go out like that!"

"Oh, honestly, Tina," her mother said.

They were standing in line at the meat counter at the supermarket when Tina saw Mrs. Glenn.

"Hello, dear." Mrs. Glenn ruffled her curls. Tina was so embarrassed to be seen with a horrible beggar woman, she couldn't even say hello back.

"How do you do?" Mrs. Glenn greeted Tina's mother as if she had never met her before. Then Mrs. Glenn's smile faded and she gasped. "Oh, dear. *Quel dommage!* What a shame. You'll have to get that fixed, *n'est-ce pas?"*

"Of course," said Tina's mother. She sounded a little impatient.

"Why don't you look for Melissa, dear," Mrs. Glenn said to Tina. "She's around here somewhere."

Tina didn't move. She just stood there staring at Mrs. Glenn.

"Sam, dear," Mrs. Glenn flashed the butcher a big smile. She fluttered her eyelashes. "The lamb chops we got last week could have been better. Now, I want some lovely lamb chops for tonight."

"Certainly, Mrs. Glenn," said the butcher.

"Sam's my boyfriend," Mrs. Glenn said to Tina's mother. "He always gives me the best cut."

Tina felt her own face turn bright red. How could Mrs. Glenn talk like that?

The butcher was showing Mrs. Glenn some freshly cut lamb chops. Mrs. Glenn fluttered her eyelashes and smiled at the lamb chops. Tina was sure Mrs. Glenn was going to kiss the lamb chops.

"Ugh," thought Tina. "How can anyone get so romantic about lamb chops?"

"Do see if you can find Melissa for me," said Mrs. Glenn. She was blowing kisses to the butcher.

Tina went off to find Melissa. She walked around the supermarket for a while, feeling very awkward.

When she came to the aisle with the cat food, she found Melissa.

Melissa was hiding behind a pile of boxes of Kitty Chow. She looked awful. Her face was bright red and her eyes were opened wide. She looked terrified. For a moment Tina thought someone must be after her.

"Shh," said Melissa, grabbing Tina and pulling her behind the Kitty Chow.

"Is my mother still talking to the butcher?"

Tina crept out and peered around the corner of the aisle. Then she tiptoed back. "Yes, she is. He's wrapping up something for her now."

"Oh, I can't stand it," wailed Melissa. "I can't stand the way she talks to people in stores. She *flirts*!"

Tina didn't blame Melissa for being embarrassed — not one bit. But she said, "Oh, she's not so bad."

"I tried to stay home," said Melissa. "But she made me come."

"Oh, Melissa, she's not so bad," Tina said again. "You ought to see my mother."

"Stay with me," whispered Melissa.

Tina was glad Melissa needed her.

A few minutes later, Tina's mother came looking for her.

"Tina — Melissa — what are you doing behind all this cat food? Come on, girls. I told Melissa's mother I'd take her to my fish shop."

"Can't we just stay here?" asked Melissa. She looked miserable.

Mrs. Glenn acted even worse at the fish market. She batted her eyelashes at Mr. Powell. Then she sighed and looked around at all the fish lying in ice.

"Oh, Mr. Powell, I need your help. You see, I'm not from around here. I was born in a small town in the Midwest. We never ate fish when I was a little girl."

"Oh, no," muttered Melissa. She and Tina were standing by the window watching the lobsters crawl around. "He doesn't want to hear her life story."

Mrs. Glenn gave another big sigh. "Now, tell me absolutely everything you can about *fish*." Mrs. Glenn looked at Mr. Powell as if he were the most fascinating man in the world.

"I can't stand it another minute." Melissa rushed out the door. Tina followed and waited outside with Melissa until their mothers came out.

Tina's mother suggested that they all stop off for an ice cream soda.

"Well, I am a bit behind in my schedule..." said Mrs. Glenn. "I guess it would be all right."

At the coffee shop, Tina and Melissa asked if they could have a table all to themselves. The coffee shop was empty and the waiter said he didn't mind.

Tina and Melissa ordered ice cream sodas. Melissa sipped hers with her hands over her ears.

"...I'm on a diet," Melissa's mother was telling the waiter. "I really shouldn't have anything fattening..."

"Oh, you're not fat," said the waiter.

"Isn't he sweet?" asked Mrs. Glenn.

Melissa rolled her eyes. "Make her stop!"

"Oh," she whispered to Tina. "My mother is so embarrassing."

"Well, what about my mother?"

"What about her?" asked Melissa in surprise.

"She's missing a tooth!" said Tina.

"Oh," said Melissa. She didn't seem very impressed.

"And why do you think I told Sarah she was my baby-sitter?" asked Tina.

"Huh?" asked Melissa.

"Why do you think I told Sarah..." Tina stopped. Was it possible that Sarah had never told Melissa? Melissa's face was blank. Tina suddenly thought Sarah was a very nice person.

"Speaking of Sarah..." said Melissa, who hadn't really been listening. "She's beginning to get on my nerves."

Tina was shocked. She couldn't say anything. But Melissa was waiting for her to say something.

"She really is beginning to get on my nerves," sighed Melissa.

"I like Sarah," Tina burst out. Then she saw a funny look come over Melissa's face. For a second Melissa looked frightened.

"Oh, of course I like her too," Melissa said.

They finished their ice cream sodas in silence. Tina glanced at her mother. To her surprise her mother no longer looked like a beggar woman; she just looked like Tina's mother with a missing tooth.

Tina suddenly felt grown-up — much more grown-up than Melissa. She was feeling very grown-up until she realized she had been blowing bubbles in her ice cream soda.

Blood Sisters

The next morning Tina woke up feeling good. She put on her black and white spotted dog costume. Mrs. Turner had told the class that they could wear their Halloween costumes to school if they wanted to.

"Don't you look sweet," her mother said. And Nathaniel barked at her all during breakfast.

When Tina got to school, she found out that no one else in her class was wearing a Halloween costume. She couldn't figure it out. Last year, everyone had come to class dressed as witches, vampires, ghosts, and robots. "This year must be different," thought Tina, wishing she had brought something to change into.

Melissa ignored her completely. Tina wondered if it was just because Melissa didn't want to be seen with someone in a dog outfit. But Tina *had* expected Melissa to be a little more friendly after their meeting the day before. "That's what I get for being so grown-up," thought Tina. "Maybe I should have let her complain about Sarah."

At lunchtime Tina just couldn't bear to sit alone in the cafeteria — not in her dog outfit — not with everyone barking at her when they passed her.

She saw an empty seat across from Sarah and Melissa and sat down. Sarah seemed pleased to see her.

"Hi, Tina," she said. "You really look sweet."

"You're the only one wearing a costume," Melissa pointed out.

"I know," said Tina.

"I wish I had worn mine," sighed Sarah. Melissa gave Sarah a dirty look.

"Oh, by the way," said Melissa to Tina, "did your mother ever get her tooth fixed?"

"She's getting it fixed today," said Tina.

"I should hope so." Melissa laughed and

looked sideways at Sarah. "She doesn't exactly look *classy*."

"She's having it fixed," Tina said again.

"C'mon, Sarah." Melissa stood up and tossed back her hair.

"I'm not finished yet," said Sarah. Sarah looked as if she wanted to stay.

Then Melissa leaned over and began whispering to Sarah.

"Oh, I forgot," said Sarah. She stood up and gave Tina an apologetic look. Then she left the cafeteria with Melissa.

Tina didn't see either Sarah or Melissa during break. She looked all over the schoolyard, but they weren't there.

Sarah and Melissa got back to class late. Mrs. Turner got angry at them. Tina was glad they were in trouble.

Tina was feeling happy until she noticed the expression on their faces. They looked so pleased with themselves. They looked as if they shared a very exciting secret.

When Melissa saw Tina staring at her, she gasped and wrapped her hand in her skirt.

Then Tina saw Melissa take her sweater off the back of her chair and put it in her lap. What was she hiding? Melissa and Sarah exchanged looks and started to giggle.

"Whatever is going on?" Mrs. Turner stopped writing on the board. She turned around and glared at Sarah and Melissa. "Do you have something to tell the class?"

They both looked down. Sarah was hiding her hand in her lap too.

"What is going on?" Mrs. Turner demanded.

Linda, the class busy-body, called out, "I know." She was the class tell-tale too. Melissa's face was bright red; so was Sarah's, but they still looked pleased with themselves.

"They are blood sisters," said Linda. "They pricked their fingers with a pin and rubbed the blood together. It's a big secret..." Linda looked at the teacher as if she expected a reward. Then she went on in a sing-song voice, "And I know why it's such a big secret..."

"Oh, do be quiet," said Mrs. Turner.

"...because they don't want Tina to know," finished Linda in a low voice. But Tina heard. So did Melissa and Sarah, who looked over at Tina to see if she had heard.

Mrs. Turner made Sarah and Melissa go to the school nurse to make sure their fingers wouldn't get infected. Tina watched them leave. She bent her head low over her workbook. Linda whispered loudly to Tina, "Don't worry. I'll be your blood sister." Tina just shook her head.

She was counting the minutes until she could be safely at home with her mother. The tail on her dog costume was uncomfortable to sit on. But Tina was thankful for the long ears. She kept using them to brush away the tears that were rolling down her cheeks.

Angela Goes Shopping

On Saturday morning Tina didn't want to get out of bed.

"Are you sick, Tiner?" whispered Angela anxiously. Tina shook her head.

"Wait right here," whispered Angela. "I know what will make you happy." She ran out of the room and returned with her arms full of stuffed animals. She stuck a black and white panda in Tina's face. "There," she said. "That'll make you happy." Tina just stared out the window.

Tina's mother came into the room.

"Mummy," said Angela desperately. "Do something!"

Tina's mother was worried about her.

"C'mon, Tina," she said. "I was planning to take you shopping today. I'll buy you a new outfit."

Tina shook her head.

"It'll cheer you up," her mother said. Her mother and Angela looked so unhappy, Tina couldn't stand it. She finally said OK and slowly got dressed.

"We'll buy you something nice." Then her mother sighed. " Although we can't really afford it."

"Oh, goody," said Angela. "We can't really afford it." Angela thought "we-can't-really-afford-it" shopping trips were the most fun.

They took a taxi to town. Tina was surprised. Her mother never wasted money on taxis.

"You really do need some new clothes," her mother said, patting her hand.

Tina's mother didn't argue with the taxi driver. She didn't sing or even hum. She was very quiet. Tina was worried about her.

"More taxi!" shrieked Angela as the taxi came to a stop in front of a big department store.

Tina stared out the window of the taxi. She had never been to a really fancy department store. Her mother usually shopped in discount stores and looked for bargains.

Angela pulled back when she saw the revolving doors at the entrance to the store. She refused to go through. Her mother tried to drag her by the hand, but Angela wouldn't let her. She just stood there watching in horror.

"They're getting chopped up!"

Tina and her mother tried to explain, but Angela wouldn't listen. They had to wait until Angela was convinced that everyone was going through in one piece.

When they were inside the store, Tina felt she had stepped into another world. Everything seemed to glitter.

Well-dressed ladies were looking at jewellery and handbags. They were trying on scarves and hats. They were testing different makeups. The air smelled of perfume.

Angela sniffed loudly. "What a funny smell." Suddenly she grabbed the sleeve of Tina's coat. "Tiner..." she whispered. She tugged harder. "Tiner!" Tina looked down. Angela was staring at something. There was a look of wonder on her face.

"The stairs are moving!" Angela whispered. Tina looked.

"Oh, that?" Tina tried to sound very grown-up. "That's only an escalator."

"Hold her hand," Tina's mother called, stepping onto the escalator.

Tina held Angela's hand tightly, but halfway up, Angela slipped away and started walking down. "Come back," Tina said. She went after Angela and took her hand again.

They rode to the third floor. Tina gazed at the people around her. She thought Angela was the only one in the family dressed for the occasion. Angela was wearing a flowered smock with a heavy, white knitted shawl and her little white shoes. Her short, dark curly hair was tied up in two bunches on top of her head. People around them looked at Angela and smiled.

Tina was wearing an old raincoat that was missing its belt.

And her mother — well, her mother looked the same as always. Even though her tooth was now fixed, she wasn't exactly *classy*, as Melissa said.

As they walked into the Pre-Teen Department, Tina was sure that no one would assist them. They might even be thrown out of the store, she thought.

"May I help you?" A saleslady greeted them. She beamed down at Angela.

"I have to go to the potty," said Angela.

"That's down on the second floor," said the saleslady. She was still smiling.

"Oh, dear," said Tina's mother. "Look, Tina,

tell the saleslady what you need. We'll be right back. Something for school," she added.

"So," said the saleslady, looking Tina up and down. "Let me show you what they're all wearing this year."

She led Tina to a corner of the Pre-Teen Department where there was a big sign that said BACK TO SCHOOL. "This little knit is our biggest item."

Tina looked at the dress. It was red, gold, and brown plaid with fake pockets and a fake belt in the back.

"It's what they're all wearing," said the saleslady.

Tina didn't know who "they" were. She had never seen anyone in a dress like that. But she wanted to be polite. She didn't want to hurt the saleslady's feelings so she tried the dress on. Then she tried on five other dresses that "everyone was wearing."

Clothes began piling up. Tina couldn't understand why her mother and Angela were taking so long.

She was standing in front of the mirror in a black velvet suit which the saleslady thought was "adorable," when she saw her mother coming up behind her. Her mother looked upset.

"Where's Angela?" Tina asked.

"She went shopping," said her mother. She looked as if she were going to cry.

"Huh?" said Tina.

"We were in the ladies' room and I was having trouble getting the toilet door open. I heard Angela washing her hands. Then she said, 'I'll be right back, Mummy. I have some shopping to do.' By the time I got out, she was nowhere to be seen."

Then Tina noticed a store guard standing behind her mother. He was listening to his walkie-talkie. "Don't worry," he said. "They always turn up."

The saleslady came over. "Your daughter has marvelous taste," she said. "Would you like to see what she's picked out?"

"Not right now," said Tina's mother. "My little one is missing."

"Oh, dear," said the saleslady. "Well, why don't you run along and find her?" She looked at Tina in the black velvet suit. "It's all right, honey. You can wear that in the store."

Tina tucked the price tag into the sleeve of

the black velvet jacket. It said $145. She followed her mother and the guard to the lift. Before they got in, the guard stopped and listened for a moment to his walkie-talkie.

"She hasn't got far," he said. "That was a report from the first floor. All the bottles of sample perfume are empty, but no one saw who did it."

"Angela!" Tina's mother looked relieved. The guard gave her a pat on the shoulder. "Don't worry, lady. She shouldn't be too difficult to sniff out."

When they got to the first floor, the store manager met them. "It's better if you wait in my office," he said kindly. "We don't want to lose the both of you too."

"Where's Angela?" Tina could tell her mother was frightened. "Didn't you find her?"

"Well," said the store manager, "not exactly. But it seems a little girl in a white shawl went into the TV and radio department and turned all the televisions to Bugs Bunny. Then she got mad at a customer for trying to change the channel."

"What floor is the TV department on?"

asked Tina's mother. Tina hoped her mother wasn't going to cry.

"The sixth floor." Tina thought the store manager looked very nice. He was tall and had a black handlebar mustache.

"Can I get you a cup of coffee?" he asked Tina's mother when they were all sitting on a big leather couch.

"No, thank you," said Tina's mother, blinking back tears.

"Everyone is alerted," the store manager said gently. "We'll find her any minute now."

But the minutes went by and Angela wasn't found. The store manager studied a floor plan of the store as more reports came in over the telephone and the walkie-talkie.

At eleven-fifteen a lady reported that a little girl was sitting in the fitting room with her, watching her try on nightgowns. When the lady went to tell someone, the little girl disappeared.

A few minutes later a report came in from the toy department. Five stuffed animals had disappeared.

Then, for the next half-hour, large stuffed

animals were seen riding up and down the escalators — all by themselves....

The descriptions of Angela changed as the morning went on:

— a little girl wearing a large felt hat.

— a little girl wearing two different high-heeled shoes.

— a little girl hopping around in a sleeping bag.

— a little girl who smelled like a walking perfume factory.

"My, she's fast," said the store manager, trying to follow Angela's trail on the floor plan.

"It's been over an hour." Tina's mother was sobbing now. Tina put her arm around her. "Oh, Tina, I wanted to cheer you up and look at me!"

Then the store manager's office became quiet — too quiet. The telephones stopped ringing and the walkie-talkie was silent. There were no reports at all. Tina suddenly felt cold all over. Where was Angela? What if she'd been kidnapped?

Tina thought about Angela and how she had tried to cheer up Tina with all her stuffed animals. Tina hadn't even paid attention, she'd been so busy feeling sorry for herself for not being a blood sister. Now her real sister was missing. What if she never saw Angela again?

The phone rang. Tina jumped. The store manager grabbed it. He looked pale. He listened for a few seconds. Then he said, "Right," and hung up. He turned slowly to face Tina and her mother.

"Well, ladies," he said. "A little girl wearing a diamond-studded dog collar is fast asleep in the furniture department." And his face broke out into a big grin.

Tina wanted to hug him.

Lunch with the Birds

Tina's mother got a terrible case of the giggles when she saw all the expensive clothes on the counter in the Pre-Teen Department.

The saleslady was very nice about the misunderstanding. She helped Tina find a pair of corduroy pants just like the ones she already had. Then everybody, including Angela and the store manager, helped Tina pick out two new blouses and some socks. Angela was holding the store manager's hand. Tina figured he was following them around to make sure they all left the store.

To her surprise, he invited them to go to lunch with him.

"We really can't," said Tina's mother, looking at her watch. She gasped. "It's already two-thirty."

"You must be starved," the store manager said.

"I am," said Angela.

"Well, then, let's go," he said. "I want to ask this young lady some questions. She really had us on a wild goose chase."

"Well," Tina's mother sighed. "That's very nice of you." Her face was flushed. Tina suddenly thought her mother looked very pretty. She wondered if the store manager thought so too.

They went to a restaurant on the top floor. It was the most beautiful restaurant Tina had ever seen. She was happy she was allowed to wear her new outfit.

There were birdcages hanging from the ceiling with bright-coloured stuffed birds in

them. The birds chirped and sang. ("It's a tape," whispered the store manager when he saw the two girls staring at the birds.) The walls were painted with pictures of tropical flowers and trees. Everyone had tiny sandwiches shaped like triangles. Tina couldn't figure out what was in them, but she thought they tasted wonderful.

Angela did most of the talking at lunch. She had lots of interesting things to say.

Tina asked her why she had red marks up and down one arm.

"That's how you put on lipstick in a store," said Angela. "I saw other people do it."

"Why do you have green marks on the other arm?" asked Tina.

"Green lipsticks," said Angela. Then she turned to the store manager, whose name was Mr. McKinney.

"Why are their clothes all pinned in the back?" she asked.

"What?" he said.

"The clothes on the big dolls."

"Oh, you mean the models. We always pin clothes on the models to make them hang right."

"And there are no sheets and blankets on

the beds." Angela was very critical. But then she sighed and said, "I just love the beds with the roofs on the top."

"I can't understand how you went up and down the escalators all by yourself without anyone seeing you." Mr. McKinney was still puzzled.

"I didn't go by myself," said Angela. "I always held somebody's hand."

Tina couldn't get over how pretty her mother looked. She never thought her mother was pretty before. She was sure Mr. McKinney thought so too. When they were waiting for dessert, he turned to her mother and said, "You look so young. I thought you were the children's baby-sitter."

Tina's mother laughed and blushed. Tina blushed too.

After they finished their desserts — chocolate pie with whipped cream — Tina's mother thanked Mr. McKinney for everything.

"It was a pleasure," he said. He looked as if he really meant it.

Tina snuggled up to her mother in the taxi. Angela was asleep on the other side.

"Mum," she said. "You know what Mr.

McKinney said about you looking like our baby-sitter?"

"Umm," her mother said.

"Well, it's the funniest thing..." Tina stopped herself. "Well, it's not the *funniest* thing." She sat up straight and stared at her mother. "It's not funny at all."

"What isn't, Tina?"

"I told Sarah you were our baby-sitter," Tina blurted out.

"Why did you do that?"

"I was embarrassed."

"For the same reason you didn't want me to go to the Parent-Teacher Conference?"

Tina nodded.

Her mother was quiet.

"Are you mad?" asked Tina.

"No," her mother said. "I'm just sorry I embarrass you."

"You don't really," said Tina. "Well, not all the time."

Her mother was thinking.

"Is that why Sarah called me Jessica?"

Tina nodded.

"Did you tell Sarah the truth?"

Tina shook her head. Then she said, "It's too

late, anyway. Sarah and Melissa are best friends."

"Oh, Tina. I am sorry."

"They're blood sisters," said Tina and she began to cry. Her mother held her tight. Tina tried not to cry too loud. She didn't want the taxi driver to hear her.

"That means forever," sobbed Tina.

"Oh, I'm sorry," her mother said. "Your father guessed that things weren't going too well between you and Melissa."

"Really?" Tina stopped crying.

"Do you have other friends?"

Tina shook her head.

"That girl on the fifth floor looks like a nice little girl."

"No!" said Tina. "I don't want anyone else for a friend." And she began to cry again very loud. She didn't care anymore what the taxi driver thought.

"I know how you feel," her mother said. "I'm sorry I said that."

While they waited at a red light, Tina told her mother about her conversation with Melissa in the coffee shop. She told her how she didn't let Melissa complain about Sarah even though Melissa might be her blood sister now, if only she had.

"It might just be a matter of time," her mother said. Then she said, "You mean Sarah never told Melissa about the baby-sitter incident?"

Tina shook her head.

"That's very unusual," her mother said.

"Very unusual," boomed the voice of the taxi driver. He had twisted around in his seat. "Little girl, take my advice," he said. "Give that Sarah girl a call when you get home."

Tina and her mother both stared at the taxi driver.

"…if you'll pardon me butting in," he said. He turned around again. The light had turned green.

Tina watched him in the mirror. He was shaking his head back · and forth and muttering to himself, "Everybody…it happens to everybody."

Tina snuggled up to her mother again. She suddenly felt very cozy.

"Mum," she said. "I think I *will* call Sarah."